A BOOK BY:

HARSHVIR SINGH KALIA

ECHOES OF THE

WHERE LEGENDS SLEEP AND SPIRITS RISE

HIDDEN WARRIOR

AF518149

BlueRose ONE.com
Stories Matter
NewDelhi • London

BLUEROSE PUBLISHERS
India | U.K.

BlueRose ONE.com
Stories Matter
NewDelhi • London

For permissions requests or inquiries regarding this publication, please contact:

BLUEROSE PUBLISHERS
www.BlueRoseONE.com
info@bluerosepublishers.com
+91 8882 898 898
+4407342408967

ISBN: 978-93-7018-045-1

Cover design: Daksh
Typesetting: Tanya Raj Upadhyay

First Edition: April 2025

TABLE OF CONTENTS

CHAPTER 1:
A CODE BETWEEN US

Aiden Reynolds wasn't much for parties. As the city roared with the energy of New Year's Eve, he found himself exactly where he'd been for the past five years: in front of his computer. His fingers moved swiftly over the keyboard, the quiet hum of the machine and comfort against the chaos outside. For Aiden, a software developer by trade, coding was more than just work—it was his refuge. The structured world of zeros and ones offered a clarity that life didn't.

It wasn't that Aiden didn't have friends. He did—two, to be exact. Jake and Eli had been his closest companions since college, and while their paths had diverged, their bond never faded. They were the ones who dragged him out for drinks on occasion, who kept him grounded when his world became consumed by work. But even with them, Aiden felt a certain distance, like he was always one step removed from the connections other people seemed to make effortlessly.

"Man, you need a pet or something," Jake said a few months ago during one of their late-night hangouts.

"Yeah," Eli agreed, slinging an arm around Jake's shoulder. "A cat would be perfect for you. Independent, low-maintenance. Won't even notice when you're glued to that screen of yours."

Aiden had laughed it off at the time, but the thought lingered. He'd never considered himself an animal person, but the idea of coming home to something other than silence gnawed at him. What would it be like to have a companion waiting for him, even if that companion was a furry, indifferent cat?

The decision to adopt didn't come easily. Aiden spent days mulling it over, weighing the pros and cons with the same methodical care he applied to coding. Was he ready for the responsibility? What if he didn't have time? What if the cat didn't like him?

But on New Year's Eve, while others celebrated the passage of time, Aiden made a choice. He found himself standing in a small, crowded animal shelter, surrounded by the sounds of soft meows and the occasional bark. He scanned the rows of cages, his heart pounding with uncertainty, until he saw him.

Curled up in a corner, his amber eyes watching the world with a quiet intensity, was a young male cat. His fur was soft and grey, and there was something about the way he held himself—calm, composed, almost regal—that drew Aiden in.

"This is Leo," the shelter worker said. "He's about a year old. Very independent, but affectionate once he warms up to you."

Leo. The name felt right. Without fully understanding why, Aiden signed the adoption papers and brought the cat home, a small part of him still wondering if he'd made the right choice.

The first few weeks were an adjustment, for both of them. Aiden's once pristine apartment quickly became littered with toys, food bowls, and cat hair. Leo was quiet, often observing Aiden with those piercing amber eyes from across the room. At night, he would curl up on the couch, his soft purrs filling the silence that had once felt so suffocating. There was something oddly comforting about having another living being in the apartment, someone who didn't demand conversation or attention, but was simply there.

Aiden found himself talking to Leo as though the cat could understand him. "Rough day," he'd say after a long coding session, Leo's tail flicking in response. In the mornings, Leo would follow him around the kitchen, meowing softly as Aiden prepared his coffee. And during those long, late nights when Aiden was knee-deep in code, Leo would sit on the desk beside him, watching the lines of text scroll by with feline curiosity.

It didn't take long for Aiden's initial doubts to fade. Leo was more than just a pet; he was a companion, someone who brought a sense of warmth and life to Aiden's otherwise solitary world. The loneliness that had once gnawed at him seemed to recede into the background, replaced by the quiet companionship of a creature who never demanded anything more than food, a warm lap, and the occasional head scratch.

As the months passed, Leo grew, both in size and in confidence. He had a way of making the apartment feel less empty, of turning the once sterile space into a home. Aiden found himself smiling more, feeling lighter in a way he hadn't in years. It was as though, without realizing it, Leo had unlocked a part of Aiden's life he hadn't known he was missing.

And then, just as everything seemed perfect, things changed.

It started one night, around midnight. Aiden had just finished up a particularly gruelling project and was about to collapse into bed when he heard it—a sharp, loud yowl that echoed through the apartment. He sat up, groggy and confused, and saw Leo standing in the middle of the living room, his fur slightly raised, his eyes wide and alert.

"What's going on, buddy?" Aiden muttered, rubbing his eyes as he walked over to the cat. But Leo didn't stop. He continued to yowl, a sound that was somewhere between a meow and a cry, his tail twitching with agitation.

Aiden figured it was a one-time thing. Maybe Leo was just feeling restless, or maybe he'd seen something outside that spooked him. But the next night, and the night after that, the yowling continued. It grew louder, more insistent, until it became an almost nightly ritual.

At first, Aiden joked about it with Jake and Eli. "I think Leo's hit puberty," he said one evening over drinks. "Must be his mating call."

They'd all laughed, imagining the once-quiet cat prowling the apartment in search of a mate. But as the nights dragged on, and the yowling became more frequent, Aiden stopped laughing. The sound was relentless, piercing the quiet of the apartment and robbing him of sleep. He found himself lying awake at night, staring at the ceiling, wondering what had changed.

Leo, once his source of comfort, was now the cause of sleepless nights and mounting frustration. No matter what Aiden did—extra playtime, new toys, late-night snacks—the yowling continued. It echoed through the apartment, a constant reminder that something was wrong, though Aiden couldn't figure out what.

And so, as the new year began, Aiden found himself at a crossroads. The bond he had once cherished now felt fragile, and the peaceful life he had built with Leo seemed to be slipping away, replaced by sleepless nights and a growing sense of unease.

Had he made a mistake?

CHAPTER 2: HOLDING ON

Aiden slumped over his desk, the glow from his computer screen casting harsh shadows on his tired face. His head throbbed with the weight of sleepless nights, the incessant noise that echoed through the apartment drilling into his mind. Another sharp yowl pierced the air, and Aiden tensed, his hands tightening into fists on the keyboard.

Leo had been yowling for weeks now, and it was wearing him down. It wasn't just the noise–it was the helplessness that gnawed at him. No matter what he did, the yowls continued, tearing through the silence, cutting into his sleep, and stealing away the peace they'd once shared.

Jake's words echoed in his mind from their last call: "Maybe he's just going through a phase, man. Cats do that, right?" But Aiden couldn't shake the feeling that something was wrong–more than just a phase. It was as though Leo was trying to tell him something, but he couldn't understand.

Aiden glanced at the clock–2:30 a.m. Another sleepless night. He stared across the room where Leo paced near the window, tail twitching, eyes wide. Aiden sighed and rubbed his temples, fighting off the dull throb of a growing headache. The thought that he might have made a mistake, that adopting Leo had been the wrong decision, began to creep in more often. But every time he looked at the cat, he couldn't bring himself to regret it fully.

The bond they'd built, the quiet companionship they had shared—it was real. He couldn't give up on that, even if he was teetering on the edge of exhaustion. But something had to change. Maybe it was time to get help. Maybe Leo was sick.

The next morning, after a particularly rough night of broken sleep and yowling that felt endless, Aiden called Jake and Eli. "I think something's wrong with Leo," he said, his voice hoarse with fatigue.

"I've never heard of a cat yowling like that for no reason," Eli said, his brow furrowing in concern over the video call. "Maybe you should take him to the vet, just to be sure."

Jake chimed in, nodding. "Yeah, man, it might be something medical. Better safe than sorry."

Aiden hesitated. He wasn't sure if it was health-related or just some behaviour issue, but the nagging worry wouldn't let him rest. What if there was something seriously wrong with Leo? The thought of not taking action, of letting something go untreated, was too much to bear.

"I'll book an appointment," Aiden finally said, swallowing the lump of anxiety that had lodged itself in his throat.

Later that afternoon, Aiden found himself sitting in the waiting room of the vet's office, his knee bouncing nervously as he held Leo's carrier on his lap. The cat was unusually quiet now, his amber eyes wide as they peered through the bars of the carrier. Aiden rubbed a thumb over the edge of the carrier, trying to calm his racing thoughts. What if it was serious? What if Leo was in pain and he hadn't noticed?

The vet, a calm and reassuring woman named Dr. Whitman, greeted Aiden with a warm smile when it was their turn. "So, what seems to be the issue with Leo today?" she asked, as she gently lifted the cat out of the carrier.

Aiden explained everything–the yowling, the sleepless nights, the growing concern. Dr. Whitman listened attentively, nodding along before beginning her examination. She checked Leo's ears, his eyes, his teeth. She felt along his spine, checked his joints, and tested his reflexes. The examination felt like it took forever, each passing second adding weight to the knot of anxiety coiling in Aiden's chest.

Finally, Dr. Whitman stood up, her expression thoughtful but calm. "Leo's perfectly healthy," she said, her tone soothing. "There's no sign of any physical issues. His heart rate is good, his weight is normal, and everything else looks fine."

Relief surged through Aiden, but it was quickly followed by confusion. "But the yowling... what's causing it?" he asked, his voice edged with frustration.

Dr. Whitman gave a sympathetic nod. "It could be behavioural. Cats sometimes go through phases of vocalizing, especially if they're feeling anxious or overstimulated. Has anything changed in his environment?"

Aiden shook his head, feeling a deep sense of helplessness. Nothing had changed—except him. He had started feeling the cracks of strain, the sleepless nights gnawing at his sanity. Was it him? Was Leo picking up on his own stress, feeding off the tension?

"Maybe he's feeling restless or needs more stimulation," Dr. Whitman suggested. "You could try some calming techniques—more interactive play, maybe even pheromone sprays to help him feel more relaxed."

Aiden thanked the vet and left the clinic with a mix of emotions. Relief that Leo was healthy. Frustration that the problem still lingered. And a growing doubt about whether he could really handle this.

That night, the yowling started again.

Aiden had tried everything—playing with Leo more, setting up new toys, and even a few calming sprays as Dr. Whitman suggested—but nothing seemed to make a difference. The noise grated against his nerves, the constant wailing becoming unbearable. Sleep continued to evade him, the sleepless nights stretching into endless weeks.

One particularly bad night, Aiden found himself standing in the living room, fists clenched at his sides as Leo's yowls echoed off the walls. His mind was foggy with exhaustion, the sharp headache that had been lurking in the background all day now pounding mercilessly at his temples.

"Leo, stop!" he shouted, his voice hoarse and filled with frustration. The cat didn't stop. The yowling continued, unrelenting.

Aiden felt a surge of anger rise in his chest, his hands trembling with the force of it. His vision blurred with fatigue and rage, and for a split second, a thought crossed his mind—an impulse, a moment of weakness where he wanted to lash out, to make the noise stop.

But then he looked at Leo—his Leo. The cat that had been his companion for the past year, the one who had brought warmth into his cold, quiet life. Leo wasn't just making noise to annoy him. He was a living creature, a part of Aiden's life that he couldn't imagine being without.

The anger faded, replaced by a flood of guilt. Aiden collapsed onto the couch, burying his face in his hands. He couldn't do it. He could never hurt Leo. The thought of it made his stomach turn. This wasn't Leo's fault, and Aiden knew it. Something was wrong, but it wasn't the cat's doing.

As the days dragged on, Aiden's health began to falter. The sleepless nights had taken their toll, and he found himself plagued by constant headaches, sometimes so intense they blurred his vision. His work suffered, his focus shattered by the exhaustion that seemed to seep into every part of his life. Migraines came and went, leaving him debilitated for hours at a time.

The doubt grew like a shadow, always lurking at the edge of his thoughts. He found himself questioning everything–had he made a mistake adopting Leo? Was he fit to care for another living being when he could barely take care of himself?

He had never thought that having a pet could be this hard. The dream of companionship, of finding solace in another life, seemed to be crumbling around him. He loved Leo, but that love was being tested every night, with every yowl that pierced through the silence of the apartment.

Aiden knew he couldn't give up on Leo—not yet. But as the days wore on, and the sleepless nights continued, a gnawing fear crept in. What if this was it? What if things never got better?

What if he had made a terrible mistake?

CHAPTER 3: THE MATING MISSION

The days stretched on, and so did Aiden's sleepless nights. The relentless yowling from Leo had become a familiar, if unbearable, soundtrack to his life. The migraines still haunted him, but one day, as he sat on the couch, half-delirious from exhaustion, a sudden thought flashed across his mind—a thought that was both absurd and strangely comforting.

Maybe Leo just needed to... well, mate.

Aiden laughed at himself at first. Was he really thinking this? But the more he considered it, the more sense it made. Leo was a young, healthy male cat. Maybe all this incessant yowling was simply nature's call, a deep primal need that Aiden, in his ignorance, had overlooked. He knew that animals had natural instincts, and maybe this was Leo's way of screaming, "Dude, I need a girlfriend!"

The idea seemed crazy, but what else could it be? "Okay, Leo," Aiden muttered to his cat, who was now staring out the window and—surprise—yowling again. "If it's love you need, it's love you're gonna get."

The next few days were nothing short of chaotic. Aiden threw himself into a new mission: Operation Find Leo a Mate. He downloaded every cat-owner app, joined local pet-owner Facebook groups, and even posted ads on classified websites.

Looking for a lady cat who's ready to mingle. Must love naps, high-quality kibble, and ignore my cat's weird yowling. Serious inquiries only.

As expected, the replies were... mixed.

One lady sent him a lengthy email detailing her cat's family lineage. "She's a purebred Persian," she wrote proudly. "Her fur is as soft as silk, and she has the most exquisite temperament. Your cat should consider himself lucky."

Another woman responded with a cat video. "Here's Mittens in action. As you can see, she's quite the dancer. Maybe Leo could take her to a ball?" Aiden rolled his eyes but replied politely.

And then there was Barry—an older gentleman who enthusiastically claimed that his cat, Trixie, was "the sassiest feline this side of town." Aiden wasn't sure if that was a selling point, but at this point, he wasn't picky.

And so began the series of awkward cat dates. The first one took place at Barry's house, where Trixie greeted Leo with all the warmth of an ice queen. She arched her back, hissed, and stalked off to sit on top of the refrigerator, glaring down at Leo like he was an uninvited guest to a royal banquet. Leo, unimpressed, wandered around sniffing the floor as if searching for invisible snacks.

"Looks like Trixie's playing' hard to get," Barry said, chuckling. "Maybe Leo's got to turn up the charm."

But Leo wasn't turning anything up. He was just walking around, giving zero attention to Trixie. Aiden scratched his head. Wasn't this supposed to be instinctual? He felt like a dad on a terrible blind date for his kid.

The next date wasn't much better. Aiden had arranged to meet Carol and her lovely Maine Coon, Fluffy. As Aiden nervously explained Leo's recent behaviour, Carol smiled sympathetically. "Oh, don't worry. Fluffy is quite the socialite. She loves meeting new cats."

Fluffy strutted over to Leo with all the confidence in the world, her luxurious tail swishing as she circled him. Leo gave her a quick glance, then promptly sat down, yawned, and started grooming his paws.

Carol blinked. "Maybe Fluffy's too forward for him?"

Aiden wanted to slam his head into a wall. Was his cat seriously rejecting every lady in the neighbourhood?

Weeks turned into months, and the situation only got funnier–and more ridiculous. Aiden found himself in absurd situations, meeting all sorts of eccentric cat owners in his quest to find the perfect mate for Leo.

There was one particularly awkward encounter when he met a woman named Susan, whose cat, Bella, was a Siamese beauty. Susan took the whole "cat matchmaking" concept to another level.

"I've set up a romantic area in the living room for them," she announced proudly as Aiden and Leo walked in. Sure enough, there were rose petals scattered on the floor, soft jazz music playing, and what appeared to be two small bowls of catnip arranged like a candlelit dinner.

Aiden stood there, speechless. Leo wandered over, sniffed the catnip for a moment, and then rolled onto his back, completely ignoring Bella, who was perched daintily on the couch, eyeing him with disdain. Bella made a half-hearted attempt to saunter over, but Leo was too busy rolling around on the floor in a catnip-induced daze.

"Is this normal for him?" Susan asked, a hint of disappointment in her voice.

Aiden sighed. "At this point, I'm not sure what's normal anymore."

After about three months of failed attempts, Aiden was ready to give up. He had presented Leo with every eligible bachelorette in the city, from fluffy Persians to sleek Bengals, but the result was always the same. Leo either ignored them, hissed back at them, or just decided he had more important things to do—like staring out the window or licking the couch cushions.

Even Jake and Eli couldn't help but laugh at the absurdity of the situation.

"Dude, it's like your cat is a professional bachelor," Jake teased one night as they sat on Aiden's couch, Leo curled up on his lap. "He's rejecting more ladies than I did back in high school."

"Yeah, maybe he's just holding out for 'the one,'" Eli added with a smirk.

Aiden shook his head, half-amused and half-frustrated. "Or maybe my cat's just destined to be single forever."

But through all the laughter, something had become painfully clear: no amount of matchmaking or romantic setups was going to solve the problem. Despite the endless parade of female cats, Leo's yowling hadn't stopped. The noise persisted, night after night, driving Aiden up the wall.

As funny as it all was, Aiden couldn't escape the creeping dread that there might be something deeper at play. After months of trying to fix it with love and laughs, the problem hadn't gone away. And now, Aiden found himself right back where he started—exhausted, confused, and helpless.

He loved Leo, but he couldn't help wondering... what if this was a sign of something else? What if the yowling wasn't about mating at all?

CHAPTER 4:
A SCEPTIC'S STRUGGLE

Aiden sat in the dimly lit corner of his living room, the flicker of the city lights outside casting long, wavering shadows against the walls. His hands trembled as he ran them through his messy hair, his eyes bloodshot from another sleepless night. Leo was curled up on the couch, unusually silent after the relentless yowling that had stretched into the early hours of the morning. The apartment was quiet now, but the silence wasn't comforting—it was heavy, like a weight pressing down on his chest.

The exhaustion had become a part of him, creeping into every thought, every action, until he felt like he was no longer himself. He had tried everything—talking to friends, going to the vet, following every piece of advice thrown his way—but nothing worked. The yowling continued, and with it, the gnawing doubt that had taken root in his mind.

His thoughts drifted back to that morning, standing in front of the bathroom mirror, staring at his own reflection. He barely recognized the man looking back at him. Dark circles clung beneath his eyes, his skin pale and drawn. The sharp throb of a migraine pounded at the base of his skull, and for the first time in his life, he felt like he was unravelling.

"You're not a good parent," a small, insidious voice whispered in the back of his mind. "You don't know how to take care of Leo. You should give him up, before it gets worse."

Aiden shook his head, trying to dispel the thought. But it was always there now, lurking at the edge of his consciousness. He had never doubted himself this much. Before Leo came into his life, everything was clear, structured. He was a man of logic and reason, raised in a world where everything had an explanation. His job as a software developer thrived on structure, precision, and clarity. Problems had solutions. Every bug had a fix. Every issue had an answer.

But this? There was no code to debug, no solution to patch. And that was driving him mad.

Later that day, Aiden sat with Jake and Eli at their usual café, the faint hum of city life buzzing around them. But today, the warmth of their friendship felt distant. He stirred his coffee absentmindedly, his eyes fixed on the dark liquid as if it could provide the answers he desperately sought.

"You look like hell, man," Jake said, his voice cutting through the haze of Aiden's thoughts. "You need to take care of yourself. It's not just about Leo."

Aiden gave a tired smile, though it didn't reach his eyes. "I'm trying, Jake. But I don't know what else to do.

I love him, but—" He stopped, the weight of the words almost too heavy to say out loud. "Maybe I'm not cut out for this. Maybe I should… I don't know, find him a better home."

Eli frowned, her eyes filled with concern. "You're not thinking straight, Aiden. You've barely slept for weeks. It's normal to feel overwhelmed."

Aiden's hand tightened around his coffee cup, his frustration bubbling to the surface. "Normal? What's normal about this?" he said, his voice sharper than he intended. "I've tried everything. The vet says he's fine. Everyone says he's fine. But he's not. And I'm… I'm not. I can't keep doing this."

"Maybe you just need a break," Eli suggested gently. "Take a few days off, clear your head. It's not about giving up—it's about taking care of yourself too."

But Aiden wasn't convinced. The doubts gnawed at him, louder than ever. He had always been so sure of himself—so sure of everything. He didn't believe in anything that couldn't be proven, that didn't have a logical explanation. He had no room in his life for spiritual nonsense, for talk of energies or entities. The world was black and white, and anything beyond that was a fairytale.

But lately, things felt different. He felt different.

That night, Aiden lay awake in bed, staring at the ceiling. Leo was at the foot of the bed, his small body curled into a tight ball. Aiden's mind raced, every thought a chaotic swirl of guilt and exhaustion. He loved Leo—he knew that much. But the love felt heavy now, tangled with frustration and fear. What if he wasn't enough? What if he couldn't handle this?

He remembered the conversation he had with his parents years ago when they had first gotten a family dog. His father had been adamant that taking on a pet was a responsibility that couldn't be taken lightly, but his mother had reassured him, saying that love would guide them through the tough moments.

But love didn't feel like enough anymore. It felt like a burden—an anchor pulling him under.

A part of him—the rational part—tried to calm his racing mind. It's just a rough patch, he told himself. You're tired. You're stressed. That's why everything feels so overwhelming. But another part of him, the part that had grown in the dark of sleepless nights and endless noise, whispered doubts. You can't do this. You're not a good parent. You'll never be able to give Leo what he needs.

Aiden's heart twisted in his chest. The guilt was unbearable. He couldn't abandon Leo—he couldn't. But what if keeping him was just as bad? What if staying meant they would both suffer?

As the days passed, Aiden's health continued to deteriorate. The migraines became more frequent, the fatigue heavier, and the thoughts darker. He had never been one to believe in anything beyond the physical world, but the strain was starting to wear down even his staunch scepticism.

It wasn't that he suddenly believed in supernatural forces or energies—he didn't. That was nonsense, wasn't it? Just something people made up to explain things they didn't understand. Aiden had always prided himself on his logical mind. There were no ghosts, no spirits, no unexplained forces at work here. Just a tired man and a frustrated cat.

But every time Leo's yowls filled the apartment, Aiden felt something shift inside him. Something uneasy, something unfamiliar.

Was it the exhaustion playing tricks on his mind? Was his body so worn down that he was starting to imagine things? He didn't know. All he knew was that his love for Leo was starting to feel like a cage. Every time he thought about finding another home for him, the guilt crushed him, but staying felt like slowly suffocating under the weight of his own failing.

Aiden had always believed that every problem had a solution. But what was the solution here? He was on the verge of collapse, his mind and body stretched to their limits. He was losing control, losing himself. And worst of all, he didn't know how to stop it.

For the first time in his life, Aiden felt truly lost.

CHAPTER 5: A HEARTBREAKING GOODBYE

Aiden sat on the edge of his bed, hands trembling as he stared at the adoption centre form lying on the table. The pen felt heavy in his hand, the weight of the decision crushing his heart. His apartment, once filled with the soft purrs of Leo and their quiet companionship, now seemed like a battleground of sleepless nights, constant loud meows, and the overwhelming guilt of feeling like he had failed as a parent.

He had tried everything–discussions with friends, countless trips to the vet, even changing his routine. But nothing seemed to work. Leo's behaviour grew more erratic, and with each sleepless night, Aiden's frustration mounted. The headaches had worsened, his work suffered, and a fog of exhaustion clouded his every thought. He loved Leo, but the burden of doubt pressed on him: Was he doing what was best for the cat? The thought gnawed at him relentlessly.

"I'm not a good parent," he whispered to himself in the quiet of the morning, the words tasting like failure. Tears welled up in his eyes, but he blinked them away. This was the right choice–for both of them.

That afternoon, Aiden placed Leo gently into his carrier. Leo didn't fight, but his eyes, once filled with playful curiosity, seemed to sense something was wrong. As Aiden carried him out of the apartment, memories flashed before his eyes like a reel he couldn't stop.

He remembered the first time he brought Leo home, that tiny bundle of fur nervously exploring the new space, only to curl up on Aiden's chest the same night, purring softly. He remembered winter mornings when Leo would snuggle close to him under the warmth of the blankets, his small paws resting gently against Aiden's heart. And those moments of quiet companionship, Leo perched beside Aiden while he worked late into the night, the cat's mere presence making everything feel just a little easier.

Each memory was a fresh wound, a reminder of the love they had shared, and now, of the goodbye he was forcing on them both. By the time he reached the adoption centre, Aiden's breath came in short, ragged gasps, each step heavier than the last.

The woman behind the desk greeted him with a kind smile, but Aiden barely heard her. His eyes remained locked on Leo, who sat quietly in his carrier, unaware of the heartbreak that was about to unfold. Aiden knelt down to say goodbye, his hand trembling as he opened the carrier's door.

For a moment, Leo didn't move. He simply looked up at Aiden, his wide, trusting eyes locking with Aiden's.

It was in that gaze that Aiden felt his heart shatter. The look was filled with love, confusion, and an unspoken question: Why are you leaving me?

Aiden choked back a sob as he stroked Leo's soft fur one last time, memories flooding him—Leo curling up beside him on the couch, nudging his hand for attention, greeting him at the door after long days. Every small gesture, every quiet moment shared, now felt like a knife twisting deeper into his heart.

"I'm sorry, Leo," Aiden whispered, his voice barely audible. "I'm so, so sorry."

As he stood to leave, the tears he had held back finally broke free, streaming down his face in a torrent. He turned away, not able to bear the sight of Leo watching him go. His chest ached, his heart torn between the guilt of abandonment and the love that had grown between them.

But as he reached the door, he couldn't help but glance back. There, inside the carrier, Leo's wide eyes followed him, silent and questioning. And in that moment, the weight of his decision crushed him completely. It wasn't just Leo he was leaving behind; it was every ounce of love, every bond they had formed, and a part of his own heart that would never be whole again.

With one final step, Aiden left the adoption centre, but the echo of that moment–the look in Leo's eyes–would haunt him forever.

CHAPTER 6: SHADOWS OF EMPTINESS

The days that followed Leo's departure were nothing short of torture for Aiden. Guilt gnawed at him relentlessly, like a parasite burrowing deeper into his mind with each passing hour. The decision to give Leo up had seemed like the only solution at the time, but now, in the stillness of his apartment, the emptiness felt suffocating. He couldn't stop thinking about the last time he saw his beloved cat, how Leo had looked back at him through the cage bars at the adoption centre, confused and scared, his wide green eyes asking why Aiden was abandoning him.

That look haunted him. He replayed it over and over in his mind. The way Leo used to curl up on his chest at night, soft and warm, purring contentedly while Aiden drifted off to sleep. The quiet companionship that the cat had offered him in his loneliest moments, the unconditional love that never demanded anything in return. Aiden had thought he was doing the right thing, sparing both of them the torment of those sleepless nights, but now he wasn't sure. Every time he closed his eyes, the memories came rushing back, flooding him with regret.

He found himself constantly questioning his decision: Had I been too selfish? Was I too weak to handle the responsibility? He knew he wasn't a perfect parent, but had he really been so bad that abandoning Leo was the only answer? The guilt was unbearable. It pressed down on his chest like a heavy weight, suffocating him, making it difficult to breathe.

His friends, Jake and Eli, tried to pull him out of the spiral. They invited him out for drinks, movies, anything to keep his mind off the emptiness. They even suggested adopting another pet or trying to reconnect with Leo through the adoption centre. But Aiden could barely muster a response. He would stare blankly at the walls of his apartment, as if waiting for the familiar soft patter of paws, the playful meow that used to greet him at the door. The apartment had never felt so silent, so eerily still.

"Come on, man," Jake urged one evening, setting a plate of food in front of him. "You've got to snap out of it. Leo's in a good place now. You did the best you could."

But the words fell flat. The guilt twisted inside Aiden like a knife. Did I really?

He tried to bury himself in work, but even that didn't help. The once comforting routine of coding, which had always provided an escape, now felt hollow. His focus wavered, his mind foggy and distracted. Every keystroke seemed to echo in the emptiness of his apartment, a reminder of how quiet everything had become. The joy he once took in solving problems, in building and creating, had drained away, replaced by a crushing sense of failure.

And then there were the physical symptoms. At first, they had been minor—just a headache here and there, a dull ache behind his eyes. But as the days dragged on, the headaches became more frequent, sharper, until it felt like his skull was being split open from the inside. His energy evaporated, and no matter how much he slept, he always woke up feeling like he hadn't rested at all. His skin, once healthy and vibrant, had grown pale, almost sickly. His clothes hung looser on him now, his body withering under the weight of stress.

But it was more than just exhaustion. Something felt wrong. Deeply, inexplicably wrong. The air in the apartment had changed. It was heavier, colder, despite the warm summer weather outside. Aiden had always been a sceptic—a firm non-believer in anything supernatural or spiritual. He lived in the world of logic and reason, a software developer who found comfort in the predictable, the explainable. But now, there was something almost... unnatural about the way his health was deteriorating.

Even his friends had noticed.

One evening, Jake sat across from him, a deep frown on his face. "Aiden, seriously, what's going on? You look like you haven't slept in weeks."

"I... I don't know," Aiden admitted, rubbing his temples as another wave of pain shot through his head. "I've been trying to rest, but... I just can't shake this feeling."

"What feeling?" Eli asked, concerned etched in his features. "Man, we're really worried about you. Something's not right."

Aiden hesitated. How could he explain it when he didn't even understand it himself? It wasn't just the guilt or the stress of giving up Leo. It was something else—something darker, lurking just beyond the edges of his awareness. The apartment felt different. Not just empty, but wrong somehow, as if the very walls were closing in on him, watching him, feeding off his despair.

"I don't know how to describe it," Aiden finally said, his voice low. "It's like... I feel like I'm being drained. Like something's sapping the life out of me."

Jake and Eli exchanged uneasy glances. They had both felt it too, though neither wanted to admit it. The air in Aiden's apartment was thick with an oppressive weight, an invisible tension that made their skin crawl.

"It's just stress, man," Jake said, though his voice lacked conviction. "You've been through a lot. Losing Leo, all those sleepless nights... it's bound to take a toll."

Aiden nodded, though deep down, he wasn't convinced. It felt like more than that. Much more. The shadows in the apartment seemed darker, the nights longer, and strange noises echoed through the halls, noises that shouldn't have been there. Every now and then, he thought he heard soft footsteps, the faint sound of claws against the hardwood floor, but when he looked, there was nothing.

His health continued to deteriorate. His pale complexion grew worse, his eyes sunken and lifeless. The headaches were now constant, pulsing and throbbing with a relentless intensity that left him barely able to function. His hands trembled, his body weak and frail, and a strange coldness settled into his bones, no matter how many blankets he piled on at night.

One morning, after another sleepless night, Aiden caught a glimpse of himself in the bathroom mirror. He hardly recognized the reflection staring back at him. His skin was sallow, almost translucent, and his eyes... they looked haunted, as if something had been slowly draining the life from him, bit by bit.

His friends rushed to his side, their concern now mixed with a growing sense of fear. They couldn't shake the feeling that something wasn't right. It wasn't just Aiden's emotional state–it was the apartment itself. The atmosphere had grown thick, oppressive, as if something unseen was lingering in the shadows, waiting.

"You need to get out of here," Eli said firmly one night. "Stay with us for a while. This place... it's not good for you anymore."

But Aiden shook his head. “Where would I go? This is my home.”

Jake placed a hand on his shoulder. “We don’t know what’s going on, but whatever it is, it’s not normal. We’ll figure this out, okay? Just... don’t give up.”

But as Aiden looked around the darkened apartment, the shadows seemed to shift and twist, and for the first time, he wondered if there was something more to all of this—something he couldn’t explain.

The walls seemed to close in, the shadows whispering secrets he couldn’t hear, and somewhere in the distance, a soft, familiar sound echoed through the stillness—the faint cry of a cat, long gone.!

CHAPTER 7: THE DESCENT

Days blurred into nights, and Aiden's world became a fog of despair. He had tried everything–seeing doctors, taking medication, talking to his friends–but nothing could shake the weight that pressed down on him. The cold emptiness of his apartment was suffocating, and the silence felt louder than any noise. He had always been a rational man, someone who didn't believe in the supernatural, but now, he wasn't so sure.

His health had deteriorated so quickly that even the doctors couldn't explain it. Physically, there was nothing wrong with him. No illness, no infection, no signs of disease. And yet, he was wasting away. He could feel his strength slipping from him, day by day. The constant headaches had become unbearable, and the shadows in his apartment seemed to grow darker, more menacing.

His friends, Jake and Eli, had become his lifeline. They visited frequently, trying to lift his spirits, but even they could sense that something was deeply wrong. The apartment felt oppressive, like a living thing, breathing down their necks, watching their every move. They never stayed for long, always finding excuses to leave after a short while, as if they too were afraid of whatever unseen force lurked in the corners of the room.

"Aiden, you have to leave this place," Eli urged one evening, his voice filled with concern. "There's something wrong here, something we can't explain."

Aiden shook his head, his eyes hollow. "Where would I go? This is my home."

Jake sighed, running a hand through his hair. "Man, this place is draining you. We're scared for you. It's not just stress. There's something else going on, and it's killing you."

Aiden wanted to argue, to tell them they were overreacting, but deep down, he felt it too. The air in the apartment was thick with an unseen presence, something dark and malevolent. He could sense it now, even if he didn't want to admit it. The rational part of his mind fought against the idea, clinging to logic, but the constant feeling of being watched, the cold that settled into his bones no matter how warm it was outside—it was undeniable.

And then there were the dreams.

At first, they were vague, fragmented memories of Leo, of his soft fur and the way he used to curl up on Aiden's lap. But slowly, the dreams grew darker, more twisted. Leo's gentle meows became haunting cries, echoing through his mind, filling him with dread. He would wake in the middle of the night, drenched in sweat, certain that he had heard Leo's voice somewhere in the apartment.

The worst part was the guilt. It consumed him, gnawing at him relentlessly. Every time he closed his eyes, he saw Leo's face, the confusion in his eyes as Aiden left him at the adoption center. The memory of that day played over and over in his mind, like a broken record, reminding him of his failure, of how he had abandoned the one creature who had loved him unconditionally.

He couldn't escape it. The guilt weighed him down, crushing his spirit, and no matter how much his friends tried to reassure him, he couldn't shake the feeling that he had made a terrible mistake.

One night, as he lay in bed, staring up at the ceiling, he heard it again—the faint sound of claws scratching against the floor. His heart raced, his pulse quickening as he sat up, straining to hear. The noise came again, soft but unmistakable, like the sound of a cat walking across the wooden floor.

"Leo?" he whispered, his voice trembling.

There was no response, only the oppressive silence of the apartment. But the feeling of being watched was stronger than ever, and Aiden could feel a cold chill crawl up his spine. He glanced around the room, his eyes darting to the shadows in the corners, half-expecting to see Leo's small form emerge from the darkness.

But there was nothing. Just the silence. And yet... he couldn't shake the feeling that something was there, lurking just out of sight, watching him.

As the days passed, Aiden's health worsened. His once vibrant face had grown gaunt and pale, his eyes sunken and hollow. He could barely eat, and his clothes hung loosely on his thinning frame. The headaches were constant now, a sharp, throbbing pain that pulsed behind his eyes, making it impossible to focus on anything for more than a few minutes at a time.

Jake and Eli grew increasingly concerned, but no matter how much they begged him to leave, Aiden refused. He couldn't abandon his home, even though it felt more like a prison with each passing day. He was trapped–trapped by his guilt, by his memories of Leo, and by the strange, suffocating presence that seemed to have taken over his apartment.

One night, after yet another sleepless night filled with nightmares of Leo's cries, Aiden stumbled into the bathroom, clutching his head in pain. He stared at his reflection in the mirror, horrified by what he saw. His skin was pale and sallow, his eyes bloodshot and sunken. He looked like a man on the verge of death.

For the first time, he admitted to himself that he was scared. Terrified, even. Something was wrong–something beyond his understanding. He had always been a man of reason, a man who believed in facts and logic, but now, standing in front of the mirror, he couldn't ignore the growing sense of dread that had taken root in his chest.

There was something in the apartment. Something dark. Something... evil.

As he stood there, staring at his reflection, he heard it again—the soft, haunting cry of a cat, echoing through the stillness of the apartment. It was unmistakable. Leo's voice, calling out to him from somewhere deep within the shadows.

Aiden's blood ran cold. He turned slowly, his heart pounding in his chest, his breath coming in short, shallow gasps. The apartment was dark, the only light coming from the dim glow of the streetlamp outside his window. But in the shadows, he could see something. A shape, small and familiar, standing just at the edge of the room.

"Leo?" he whispered, his voice shaking.

The figure didn't move, but Aiden could feel its eyes on him, watching, waiting.

He took a step forward, his heart pounding in his chest, his pulse racing. But as he reached out, the figure dissolved into the darkness, leaving only the cold, suffocating silence behind.

Aiden collapsed to the floor, his body trembling, tears streaming down his face. He couldn't take it anymore. The guilt, the fear, the growing sense of helplessness—it was all too much. He had to do something. He had to get Leo back.

But deep down, he knew it wasn't that simple. Something else was at play here, something far beyond his understanding. And as the shadows closed in around him, he realized that whatever it was, it wasn't going to let him go.

CHAPTER 8: SHADOWS IN THE LIGHT

Aiden's guilt weighed heavily upon him as the days passed without Leo. No matter how hard he tried to move on, the absence of his beloved companion gnawed at his soul. His friends had come over, tried to lift his spirits, but nothing seemed to break the hollow silence that now filled his home. The once lively space now felt like a prison—a place where Aiden's regret festered and grew.

Despite the kind words and concern from his friends, Aiden's health began to falter. It was as though something inside him was unravelling. His face turned pale, his body weak. Sleep became a distant memory, and a cold unease settled in his bones. His friends noticed the change—something unnatural was happening to Aiden. They, too, began to feel uneasy in his house, as if the shadows had taken on a life of their own.

But for Aiden, the true darkness had begun months before, long before he ever considered giving Leo up for adoption.

It had all started at the café.

Aiden had taken Leo out for a quiet afternoon, as he often did. Leo, content in his arms, seemed at peace with the world, his soft purring a familiar comfort. But something felt off that day, a strange tension hung in the air. Aiden noticed a man standing across the street, staring at them with an unnerving intensity. At first, Aiden had thought nothing of it—just someone admiring his cat. But as the minutes passed, the man's gaze remained fixed, dark and unsettling.

Aiden shifted uncomfortably in his seat, trying to ignore the creeping feeling that something wasn't right. But when he glanced back toward the street, the man was no longer there.

Instead, he was standing right next to Aiden.

The stranger's sudden appearance made Aiden's heart race, his presence almost suffocating. He was tall, cloaked in dark clothing, and his eyes—those cold, empty eyes—were locked on Leo. Without saying a word, the man reached out and placed a hand on Aiden's shoulder, his touch sending a chill through him.

"You're lucky to have him," the man said softly, his voice low and filled with an unsettling familiarity.

Aiden, confused and slightly unnerved, managed a weak smile. "Uh, thanks..."

The man's eyes lingered on Leo for a moment longer before he stepped away, disappearing into the crowd as quickly as he had come. There was something about the encounter that left Aiden feeling uneasy, but he couldn't place why. The words echoed in his mind—you're lucky to have him—but Aiden had shaken it off, telling himself it was just a strange coincidence.

He couldn't have known that the man wasn't just some passerby, admiring his cat. No, that man had known Leo's secret.

~

That night, Aiden woke to the sound of loud yowling. Leo, normally so calm and quiet, was pacing the floor, his fur on end, his eyes wide with a fear Aiden had never seen before. The noise was relentless, and Aiden, still groggy from sleep, had tried to calm him down.

"Leo, what is it? What's wrong?" Aiden whispered, kneeling beside him. But no matter how much Aiden tried to comfort him, Leo wouldn't stop. The yowling continued, echoing through the house like a warning of something unseen.

What Aiden couldn't see—what no human could—was the truth of what was happening. Leo wasn't just a regular cat. He was a being from another realm, a race known as the Felron—guardians of the cosmic balance, creatures of immense power who had taken on the form of ordinary cats to hide their true identity in the human world.

In his true form, Leo was a magnificent creature—a towering, muscular figure with large, radiant wings, covered in shimmering armour that glowed with otherworldly light. His face, though still feline, bore the wisdom of centuries, and his strength was unparalleled. The Felron had come to Earth long ago to protect humanity from unseen threats, blending into the fabric of everyday life while guarding the balance between worlds.

But now, that balance was under attack.

The man from the café—his name was Velkar, a sorcerer who had delved into forbidden arts—had recognized Leo for what he truly was. Velkar sought the power of the Felron, a power that could grant him dominion over both the human and cosmic realms. He had known that Leo's strength was tied to his bond with Aiden, a bond forged through love and trust, one that made Leo's powers even greater.

Velkar had come to break that bond.

Later that night, after Aiden had fallen asleep once more, Velkar returned, slipping silently into the house. Leo, sensing the intrusion, had unleashed his true form, confronting Velkar in the darkness. His massive wings filled the room, his armoured body glowing with celestial light.

"You know why I'm here," Velkar hissed, his voice dripping with malice as he stood before the towering figure of Leo.

Leo's eyes narrowed. "You won't succeed," he growled, his voice deep and resonant. "I am bonded to Aiden. You cannot break that bond."

Velkar smiled, his lips curling into a cruel sneer. "I don't need to break it," he replied, his eyes gleaming with dark intent. "I just need to weaken it."

With a flick of his hand, Velkar summoned a shadow—a dark, twisting entity that slithered across the floor like a living nightmare. The shadow crept toward Aiden, unseen by human eyes but pulsing with malevolent energy. Leo's wings spread wide as he prepared to fight, but Velkar had already disappeared into the night, leaving the dark entity behind.

From that moment on, the shadow had been a constant presence in Aiden's home, feeding off his energy, draining his life force bit by bit. Leo had fought valiantly to protect him, but the bond between them had already begun to weaken. The yowling that woke Aiden night after night was Leo's desperate attempt to fend off the darkness, to keep the shadow from consuming his beloved human.

But Aiden couldn't see the battle that raged around him. He could only feel its effects—the fatigue, the weight of despair that pressed down on him every day. And as the days turned into weeks, the shadow grew stronger, and Aiden grew weaker.

CHAPTER 9: THE SILENT PROTECTOR

Leo had fought valiantly, night after night, battling the entity that Velkar had left behind. The dark force, born of shadows and malice, sought to corrupt, to drain the life force from Aiden and break the sacred bond between them. But Leo–noble, fierce, and unyielding–never faltered. His wings, now spread wide in their full celestial glory, beat against the dark presence that loomed like a poisonous fog over their home. His claws, glowing with the ethereal light of the Felron, sliced through the darkness, keeping it at bay.

To Aiden, though, these nights were a blur of unsettling noises–yowls and cries that echoed through the walls of his apartment, shaking him awake. All he could hear were Leo's desperate, haunting yowls. But to him, they were cries of distress, frustration, or some unknown feline need. Aiden would rise from his bed, walk to the living room where Leo paced and yowled, and stand helplessly, unable to understand what his companion was going through.

That was the heartbreaking reality–Aiden couldn't see what was happening. He couldn't see the epic battle that took place just beyond the veil of human perception. All he could feel was a growing sense of unease, a darkness that hung around him like a cloud. He began to question everything—the bond he thought he had with Leo, the life they shared, and his ability to care for the cat he loved. He felt himself slipping into doubt, unable to make sense of the chaos that now enveloped his home.

This is what it means to be human, Leo had thought to himself many times, mid-battle, as the dark entity shrieked and lunged at him. *When they cannot see or understand something, their belief starts to waver. They doubt what they cannot comprehend, and even the purest love can be questioned.*

But Leo had never doubted. Not once.

Through every strike, every shadow that lunged at Aiden, every brush with darkness, Leo had stood firm in his love and loyalty to Aiden. His bond with Aiden was forged in something far stronger than doubt—it was made of love, trust, and protection. No amount of shadow could shake Leo's confidence in their connection. He had never believed, even for a second, that Aiden would abandon him, that the human who had taken him in, loved him, and cared for him would ever cast him aside.

Leo had fought not just for Aiden's life but for their bond, for the love that tied them together across the realms. Night after night, he endured, taking on the full force of the dark entity to protect Aiden, even when Aiden couldn't see him for who he truly was.

In the present day, Aiden sat with his friends, Jake and Eli, in his living room. The once vibrant, energetic man now looked like a shadow of himself–pale, weakened, and haunted. His friends had noticed the toll the last few months had taken on him, and they were no longer willing to sit by and watch him fade away.

"Aiden, we need to talk," Jake said softly, leaning forward. His tone was gentle, but there was a firmness to it. "It's been weeks since you gave Leo up. I know you're hurting. But... we think it's time you brought him back."

Aiden's eyes widened slightly, and his heart thudded painfully in his chest at the mention of Leo. He hadn't let himself think about it much, not since the day he left Leo at the adoption centre. It was too painful, and the guilt that lingered in the pit of his stomach gnawed at him every day. His hands trembled slightly, and he quickly clenched them into fists to steady himself.

"Bring him back?" Aiden repeated, his voice weak, as though the words themselves were too heavy to say.

"Yes," Eli chimed in, her expression soft but filled with concern. "Look, Aiden, I know you're scared. You've been through a lot. We all know how much you love Leo, and that's exactly why you need to bring him back."

Aiden stared at the floor, his thoughts swirling. Joy, guilt, and confusion crashed over him like waves. Part of him lit up at the thought of seeing Leo again–of holding him, of hearing his soft purrs. But there was something darker inside him, a fear he hadn't voiced. How could he face Leo after everything? After abandoning him? What if Leo didn't forgive him?

"I… I don't know if I can," Aiden murmured, his voice thick with emotion. "What if I'm not a good parent? What if… what if Leo doesn't want to come back?"

Jake shook his head, his voice firm but kind. "Aiden, that's not true. You did what you thought was best at the time. But you need to stop punishing yourself for it. Leo loves you. You didn't lose that bond just because you made a hard decision."

Eli leaned in closer. "Leo never gave up on you, Aiden. He's been by your side from the start, through everything. Don't you think he'd want to be with you now, even more than before?"

Aiden swallowed hard, his throat tight. He wanted to believe it. He wanted to believe that Leo would still love him, still want to come home. But the doubt lingered, that same doubt that had plagued him for months. He had made a mistake—how could Leo forgive him?

"I don't know how to face him," Aiden admitted, his voice barely above a whisper. "I don't know if I deserve him."

Jake's voice softened. "You deserve him, Aiden. And he deserves you. The bond you two have... it's not something that breaks easily. Leo hasn't stopped loving you. He never would."

Aiden's heart clenched as he thought back to all those nights—nights when Leo had yowled, and he had felt helpless, not understanding what was happening. He had doubted the bond, questioned everything, but he hadn't known. He hadn't known that Leo had been fighting for him all along.

The weight of that realization hit him hard. Tears pricked at the corners of his eyes, and he blinked them away. "Do you really think... do you think I could bring him back?"

Eli reached out and gently squeezed Aiden's hand. "Yes, Aiden. You can bring him back. And when you do, you'll see—he never stopped believing in you."

Aiden nodded slowly, feeling a spark of hope ignite in his chest. He still didn't know how he would face Leo, how he would make up for everything. But one thing was clear—Leo had never doubted their bond. And maybe, just maybe, Aiden could start believing in it again too.

CHAPTER 10: THE REVELATION

The morning sun pierced through Aiden's bedroom window, gently waking him from a restless sleep. After weeks of inner turmoil and guilt, today was the day he would finally bring Leo back home. The weight of his decision to leave Leo behind at the adoption centre had been unbearable, gnawing at his heart, but this morning, a fragile sense of hope had returned.

In the kitchen, Jake and Eli sat at the table, quietly sipping their coffee as Aiden joined them, the tentative smile on his face a sign of something long missing—determination.

"You ready to bring Leo home?" Jake asked, his voice warm but serious.

Aiden nodded, a flicker of excitement in his eyes. "I have to. I should have never let him go."

Eli gave him a reassuring smile. "He's been waiting for you. I'm sure of it."

The trio left the apartment and piled into the car, the tension hanging in the air slowly beginning to ease. As they drove toward the adoption centre, Aiden's mind drifted to the many memories he had with Leo. A reel of images played in his head—Leo curling up in his lap, Leo's gentle purring that filled the silence of long nights, the bond they had shared that was so much more than just pet and owner.

Aiden smiled faintly, remembering the first time he'd brought Leo home. How nervous he had been about whether adopting a cat was the right choice, and how quickly Leo had become the centre of his world. But guilt gnawed at the edges of his thoughts. *How could I have abandoned him?* The question lingered in his mind as they approached the adoption centre.

Stepping inside, the familiar smell of pet food and disinfectant filled Aiden with nervous energy. The receptionist behind the desk offered a polite smile as Aiden explained why he was there. But as soon as she recognized his name, her expression changed, a look of discomfort crossing her face.

"Mr. Reynolds," she said quietly, "we need to talk. Could you follow me to the office?"

Aiden's heart sank. He glanced at Jake and Eli, worry tightening in his chest. "What's wrong?"

The receptionist led them into a small room and gestured for them to sit. "It's about Leo," she began, her voice soft but serious. "I'm afraid he's no longer here."

The words hit Aiden like a physical blow. "What do you mean? Was he adopted by someone else?"

"No," she replied, shaking her head. "He disappeared."

Aiden blinked, confusion overtaking him. "Disappeared? How?"

She sighed, leaning forward slightly. "The day after you left him, Leo wasn't himself. He stopped eating, didn't respond to any of us, and he spent all his time staring at the door, as if waiting for someone. We tried everything—his favourite treats, toys—but nothing worked. He seemed... terrified."

"Terrified?" Aiden repeated, his stomach twisting with guilt.

The receptionist nodded. "It was as though he was afraid of something, or waiting for you. Then one morning, when we went to check on him, he was gone."

Jake leaned forward. "Gone? How can a cat just disappear from a secure facility?"

The receptionist frowned. "We don't know. We searched the entire centre and found no sign of him. His collar tracker was found on the floor near the back exit, but it doesn't make sense. The doors were locked, and there were no signs of a break-in. It's as if he vanished into thin air."

Aiden felt sick, his mind reeling. *Leo was terrified. He needed me, and I wasn't there.*

Eli placed a comforting hand on Aiden's arm. "Do you think someone could have taken him?"

The receptionist shook her head. "We considered that, but there were no signs of a break-in or tampering with the enclosure. We've never seen anything like it."

Aiden stood abruptly, pacing the small room as his mind raced. *Leo was trying to get back to me. He was afraid because something was wrong–because something was in my home.*

"Thank you for telling me," Aiden said, his voice low and tight. "If you hear anything... anything at all, please let me know."

As they left the centre, Aiden felt a crushing sense of guilt. *Leo had been waiting for me, and I wasn't there for him.* But beyond the guilt, something else gnawed at him–a growing certainty that Velkar, the strange man he had encountered months ago, was involved in all of this.

That night, Aiden sat alone in his darkened apartment, guilt and confusion swirling through his mind. The apartment felt cold, suffocating, as though the very air had turned against him. *Leo, where are you?*

Suddenly, a faint sound broke through the silence–a yowl. Aiden froze, his heart pounding. *Was that... Leo?*

"Leo?" he whispered, rushing to the window. He peered out into the empty street, but saw nothing. Yet, the yowl came again, clearer this time, more insistent. Without hesitation, Aiden grabbed his coat and keys, hurrying outside and following the sound.

The yowling led him through winding streets, past silent houses, until it stopped in front of an abandoned building. The facade was crumbling, overtaken by ivy, and a shiver of unease crept down Aiden's spine as he stepped through the door.

"Leo?" Aiden called into the dark, his voice echoing in the emptiness.

A shadow moved in the corner of the room. Aiden's breath caught in his throat as Leo emerged from the darkness–but this wasn't the Leo he knew.

Aiden's eyes widened in disbelief as Leo's small feline body shimmered, transforming before his eyes. Leo's figure expanded into something grand, majestic, otherworldly. His wings–massive and gleaming with an ethereal light–unfurled, and his body, muscular and armoured, glowed with a radiant power. His eyes, though still feline, gleamed with ancient wisdom.

Aiden stumbled backward, his heart racing. "L-Leo?"

The creature–no, the guardian–stepped forward, his voice deep and resonant. "Aiden."

Aiden's mind swirled with questions, confusion, and awe. "What... what are you?"

Leo's voice remained steady, his eyes glowing softly. "I am Felron, a guardian from another world. I was sent here to protect you."

Aiden's breath came in ragged gasps, disbelief crashing over him. "Protect me? From what?"

"From the darkness that seeks to consume you," Leo explained, his voice filled with both strength and warmth. "I've fought for you every night, shielding you from the dark entity Velkar left behind."

Aiden shook his head, tears stinging his eyes. "The yowling... the noise every night... you were fighting something? And I never knew?"

"Yes," Leo said. "You couldn't see it, but I've been fighting to protect you. Velkar, the man you met months ago, seeks to sever our bond and claim my power."

Aiden felt a wave of guilt and awe crash over him. "I thought you were just... I thought I wasn't a good enough owner. I thought I failed you."

Leo's gaze softened. "You never failed me, Aiden. Our bond is forged from love, and I never doubted you—not even for a moment."

Tears spilled from Aiden's eyes as he looked at Leo, this magnificent being who had stood by him, protected him, and loved him, even when Aiden hadn't understood. "I... I'm so sorry."

Before Leo could respond, a sinister laugh echoed through the room, sending a chill down Aiden's spine.

Velkar stepped out from the shadows, his dark eyes gleaming with malevolent delight. "So the human finally sees the truth."

Aiden's blood ran cold. "Velkar," he whispered.

Leo stepped forward, his wings spreading protectively. "You will not harm him, Velkar."

Velkar sneered, dark energy swirling around his hands. "Oh, but I already have. The bond between you is weakened, and soon, it will be severed for good."

CHAPTER 11: THE BATTLE FOR THE BOND

The air crackled with tension as Velkar summoned his dark forces, the shadows around him twisting and writhing like living nightmares. Aiden stood behind Leo, his heart racing, but there was a surge of strength within him—something that came from the bond he shared with Leo. He wouldn't run. Not this time.

Velkar's eyes glinted with sadistic joy as he sent a torrent of dark energy toward Leo, the air humming with the force of his attack. Leo roared, his wings unfurling, and with a mighty sweep, he deflected the dark energy with a shield of light. The clash of forces shook the very foundations of the building.

Leo charged, his armoured body glowing with power, claws slashing through the shadowy minions Velkar had summoned. The battle was fierce, raw, and brutal. The entity, once hidden in shadows, now fought in the open, slashing at Leo with tendrils of dark energy. Each blow landed with a sickening thud, sending sparks of light and shadow clashing in midair.

Aiden watched in awe, his heart pounding as Leo fought like a warrior from another world, his every move graceful yet deadly. But Velkar was relentless, his power swelling with each passing moment.

"This is what you chose to protect, Leo? A fragile human?" Velkar sneered, hurling another blast of energy.

Leo's wings flared, shielding Aiden from the attack. "You will not break us," he growled. "Our bond is forged in love. You cannot sever it."

Velkar's laughter echoed through the room. "Love? Love is weak. It makes you vulnerable."

But as Leo deflected the next attack, something shifted. Aiden, standing behind his guardian, felt a surge of warmth flow through him. It was as though the bond between them was coming alive, strengthening with every moment they stood together. He could feel Leo's power, his strength, and it wasn't just the guardian protecting the human–it was both of them, working as one.

Aiden stepped forward, no longer afraid. "You're wrong, Velkar. Love is the strongest force there is."

Together, Aiden and Leo unleashed a wave of energy–a powerful, radiant force that tore through the darkness, pushing Velkar back. The dark sorcerer screamed, his form distorting as the light enveloped him, burning through the shadows he had cloaked himself in for so long.

"No!" Velkar howled, his voice filled with rage and disbelief as the light consumed him. "This cannot be!"

With a final surge of power, Leo struck, his claws glowing with cosmic energy. The force of the blow shattered the dark entity within Velkar, sending him crashing to the ground. The shadows dissipated, leaving only silence in their wake.

Panting, Leo turned to Aiden, his glowing eyes filled with pride. "We did it."

Aiden, still reeling from the battle, managed a shaky smile. "Yeah... we did."

As the dust settled, the bond between them pulsed with newfound strength—no longer weakened by doubt, but fortified by the love and trust they shared.

Leo's form shimmered as he returned to his smaller, feline appearance, his eyes still holding the ancient wisdom of the guardian he was. "The battle may be over, but the bond we share will always protect us."

Aiden knelt beside Leo, resting a hand gently on his head. "I'll never doubt you again."

In the aftermath of the battle, the world outside felt calmer, lighter, as though the oppressive weight that had haunted Aiden for months had finally lifted. And as they returned home, Aiden knew that no matter what challenges lay ahead, they would face them together—stronger, united, and unbreakable.

CHAPTER 12: A MOMENT OF PEACE

For the first time in what felt like an eternity, Aiden walked into his apartment with Leo cradled safely in his arms, a sense of warmth and relief spreading through him. It was almost surreal—after all the darkness, fear, and guilt, they were finally together again. Leo, now curled up in his familiar small, feline form, purred softly, his eyes bright with contentment. The weight that had hung heavily over Aiden's life had lifted. They were home, and that was all that mattered.

As Aiden set Leo down on the couch, he couldn't help but marvel at the tiny creature before him, the same cat he had loved and cared for—and yet so much more. Leo wasn't just his cat anymore; he was a guardian, a being from another world with cosmic powers. The questions swirled in Aiden's mind—about Leo's true nature, about the world he came from, and about their bond. But for now, those questions could wait. What mattered most was that they were both here, safe and happy.

Aiden stretched and yawned. "Feels good to be back, huh, Leo?"

Leo purred in agreement, his small body curling up comfortably on the couch. His golden eyes glistened as he watched Aiden move around the room, his tail twitching lazily.

It felt like they were reclaiming a part of their old life—a life filled with warmth, laughter, and peace. Aiden smiled as he flopped onto the couch next to Leo, gently scratching behind his ears. "I have so many questions for you, but right now... I just want to enjoy this."

Leo, though silent in his cat form, nuzzled Aiden's hand affectionately, his purrs vibrating against Aiden's chest. The bond between them was stronger than ever.

The next morning, Aiden woke feeling more rested than he had in months. His body felt lighter, his mind clearer, and the dread that had weighed him down for so long had all but disappeared. For the first time in ages, he felt whole.

Leo, in his usual cat-like fashion, had spent the night nestled at Aiden's feet. As Aiden stretched lazily, Leo padded over, purring softly.

"Morning, buddy," Aiden murmured, scratching Leo's head affectionately. "I slept like a baby."

Leo meowed in response, his golden eyes bright and knowing.

Aiden showered, dressed, and went about his morning routine with a bounce in his step. Life, for once, felt normal. Well, as normal as it could with the knowledge that his cat was actually a powerful, otherworldly guardian. But Aiden had decided to keep that secret—for now. Jake and Eli didn't need to know the truth. At least, not yet.

A little while later, Jake and Eli knocked on the door. They were greeted by Aiden's usual smile—one they hadn't seen in a long time. The three of them laughed and joked as they gathered in the living room, catching up on everything that had happened over the past few weeks.

"Dude, you look like a new man!" Jake said with a grin, throwing a casual punch at Aiden's shoulder.

"Yeah, where'd this burst of energy come from?" Eli teased, raising an eyebrow. "What happened to the stressed, pale version of you?"

Aiden chuckled, glancing at Leo, who had perched himself on the back of the couch, his tail swaying happily. "I guess I just needed to recharge. You know, take a break from all the crazy."

"Well, whatever you did, it worked," Jake said, laughing. "You look like you're ready to take on the world again."

The group bantered back and forth, pulling each other's legs, making ridiculous jokes that sent them all into fits of laughter. The lightness in the room was palpable, and Leo watched it all from his spot, content and happy to see his human, Aiden, surrounded by love and joy once more.

"By the way," Eli said with a smirk, "I heard you've been killing it at work. Word on the street is you got some sort of award or something?"

Aiden grinned sheepishly. "Yeah, well, I've been in a good headspace lately. It's nice to actually focus on work again and not... you know, everything else."

Jake let out a low whistle. "Look at you, back on top of the world!"

The conversation turned light-hearted again, filled with laughter and the warmth of friendship. Leo sat quietly, watching, his heart full as he observed his human, now full of life, energy, and happiness. It was all Leo had wanted–for Aiden to be happy, to be whole.

Over the next few days, life seemed to return to a beautiful rhythm. Aiden was back to work, his focus sharper than it had been in months. His performance improved dramatically, and he soon received an award for his outstanding contributions at the office. He had never felt better–his energy was back, his enthusiasm for life rekindled, and the weight of guilt and trauma had lifted from his shoulders.

At night, Aiden slept soundly, like a man at peace, his body and mind finally allowed to heal from the chaos that had engulfed his life. And each morning, he awoke with Leo curled up beside him, their bond stronger than ever.

But in the back of his mind, there was still one thing Aiden couldn't shake—his curiosity about Leo. About who he truly was. About the world he came from. There was so much more he didn't know, and though the questions lingered, they didn't come from a place of fear. They came from a place of wonder.

One evening, as the sun set and the apartment was bathed in a soft, golden light, Aiden sat on the balcony, a cup of coffee in hand, Leo resting by his side. The sky was painted with hues of pink and orange, the air cool and calm. It was the perfect moment—peaceful, serene.

Aiden glanced at Leo, his curiosity bubbling to the surface. "Leo," he began softly, "do you think you could... show me your true form again?"

Leo lifted his head, his golden eyes shimmering in the fading light. With a soft meow, his body began to shift, the small cat form fading as his true self emerged—majestic, powerful, and radiant. The transformation never ceased to amaze Aiden. The sheer presence of Leo's Felron form took Aiden's breath away every time.

As Leo stood before him, tall and regal, Aiden couldn't help but smile. "I know we've been through a lot," Aiden said, his voice filled with awe. "But I can't help it. I have so many questions."

Leo tilted his head slightly, his deep voice filling the space between them. "I will answer what I can."

Aiden leaned back in his chair, gazing up at the powerful guardian standing before him. "Tell me about your world, about the Felron. I want to know more–about you, about where you come from."

Leo's wings stretched slightly, catching the last rays of the setting sun. "The Felron are guardians," Leo began. "We are beings of light, tasked with protecting the balance between realms. Our world, *Astoria*, exists parallel to this one, a place where light and energy flow freely. Each of us is sent to a different realm to guard and protect those we are bonded with."

Aiden's eyes widened. "So you were sent here... to protect me?"

Leo nodded. "Yes. Your soul called out, and I answered. We are bonded by more than just companionship, Aiden. Our connection goes deeper–it is tied to the fabric of the cosmos itself."

Aiden's mind swirled with wonder. "So... when you were fighting the dark entity, it wasn't just about protecting me physically. It was about protecting our bond."

"Exactly," Leo said. "Velkar sought to sever that bond because without it, my powers would have been vulnerable to him."

Aiden stared at Leo in awe, a newfound understanding washing over him. "I had no idea. I mean,

I always knew there was something special about you, but this... this is incredible."

Leo's eyes softened as he looked at Aiden. "You have always been special to me, Aiden. That is why I fight for you. Why I protect you."

Aiden smiled, feeling a warmth in his chest that he hadn't felt in a long time. "I'm glad you're here, Leo. I don't know what I would have done without you."

Leo folded his wings back gently, a soft glow surrounding him. "And I, too, am glad to be with you."

As the stars began to twinkle in the night sky, Aiden leaned back, looking up at the vastness of the universe. The questions that had lingered in his mind seemed less pressing now. He was at peace, knowing that the bond he shared with Leo was stronger than anything that could threaten them.